X

Kennedy, Richard

Come again in the
spring

DATE			
JAN 27 '78	DEC 21 '83	MAR 18 '84	
FEB 1 7 '78		NOV 27 '84	
APR 21 '78	MAR 25 '85	JAN 2	
DEC 22 '78	JUN 4 '85		
MAR 16 '79	JUN 7	OCT 10 '06	
MAY 18 '79			
MAY 23 '80	OCT 18 '86		
SEP 5 '80	NOV 4 '88		
MAR 13 '81	APR 28 '89		
FEB 11 '83	DEC 11 '90		
	APR 17 '90		

COME AGAIN IN THE SPRING

COME AGAIN IN THE SPRING

COME AGAIN IN THE SPRING

by Richard Kennedy
pictures by Marcia Sewall

Harper & Row, Publishers
New York, Hagerstown, San Francisco, London

COME AGAIN IN THE SPRING
Text copyright © 1976 by Richard Kennedy
Illustrations copyright © 1976 by Marcia Sewall
All rights reserved. No part of this book may be used or repro-
duced in any manner whatsoever without written permission ex-
cept in the case of brief quotations embodied in critical articles and
reviews. Printed in the United States of America. For information
address Harper & Row, Publishers, Inc., 10 East 53rd Street, New
York, N.Y. 10022. Published simultaneously in Canada by Fitzhenry
& Whiteside Limited, Toronto.
FIRST EDITION

Library of Congress Cataloging in Publication Data
Kennedy, Richard.
    Come again in the spring.

    SUMMARY: An old man tries to outsmart Death with
help of the birds who come to his cabin.
    [1. Death—Fiction] I. Sewall, Marcia.
II. Title.
PZ7.K385Cm   [Fic]   76-3830
ISBN 0-06-023128-9
ISBN 0-06-023129-7 lib. bdg.

For my brother Don, and for Sally,
and for Connie and Brian

R.K.

In memory of my grandparents,
George and Belle Osgood

M.S.

Snow was on the ground. Old Hark was standing out to the side of his cabin, scattering handfuls of cracked corn and scratch to the birds all around him. Now and then he sniffed the air. It smelled like more snow was coming.

A solitary figure bundled in a great bearskin coat trudged along the forest path to the old man's cabin.

He stopped in front of the
cabin and shifted a large ledger out from under his arm.
The burly figure opened it to
a page, looked at the cabin
and then to the page again,
and walked out toward the
old man.

"Good day," said the
stranger.

"Howdy," said Old Hark,
brushing his hand on his coat.
"Your face is easy, but I can't
recollect the name. We met?"

"Not in any formal way," said the stranger. "But I've passed this way before. Maybe you've caught a glimpse of me. I'm Death."

The old man straightened his back and held the feed bag a little closer to his chest.

"Death, eh? Well, you got the wrong place."

"No," Death said, opening the ledger. "You're Old Hark, aren't you?"

"Maybe, and maybe not," said Old Hark, turning his back and scattering a handful of feed.

"Well, certainly you *are*," Death said, taking a pen from his pocket. "It's all right here in the book."

"Don't give a dang what's in the book," said Old Hark. "I ain't going. Come again in the spring."

Death sighed, and took the cap off the pen. "How tiresome," he said. "Everyone tries to put it off, and all it amounts to is making a little check mark after your name." He poised the pen above the book.

Old Hark turned. "I ain't afraid of you."

"No?" Death said, looking up.

"Come again in the spring. I won't hinder you none then. But you see all these birds? Come winter time, they depend on me to feed them. They naturally ought to fly south in the fall but don't, reason that I been feeding 'em all winter since I was no bigger 'an a skip bug. They'd die if I was gone—they ain't real wintering birds. But you come back in the spring, and they'll know I won't be here next winter and have enough sense to go south."

"Oh, that wouldn't do at all," Death said. "The book is all made up in advance. Why, re-scheduling you into the springtime would take a good week's work. Erasures would have to be made, new entries, changes of address, causes of departure . . . very complicated, no trifling matter at all, I assure you. No, it really won't do at all."

"Don't know about that,"
Old Hark said, "but I ain't
going." He took a few steps
away. Death followed him.

"See here," Death said per-
suasively, "you're really getting quite old and feeble, you
know, quite past the age I
usually visit people."

"Ain't going," Old Hark
said.

Death saw that the old man was resolute, not at all in the correct state of mind for the business at hand. He considered that he might cause a tree to fall on the old man's head. He consulted his book. Next to Old Hark's name was written: "Means of departure: Quiet, gentle, peaceful." So violence was out of the question.

Death turned a page in the book and studied the entries.

"Now, look," Death said. "I can give you another day. I can fit you in for tomorrow, but then you'll have to come quietly, gently, and peacefully. Even so I'll have to stay up half the night juggling these entries, but I'll do it as a special favor."

"Not tomorrow, either," said Old Hark. "Come again in the spring."

Death was getting impatient. "You're so old now and so feeble and your memory is so shabby you won't even remember me by then, and we'll have to go through all this again."

"There ain't nothing wrong with my memory."

"Isn't there, now?"

"It's perfect."

Death smiled. "If you think so, let me make you a wager."

"Let's hear it," said Old Hark.

"It's this," said Death. "Just so I can be sure you'll remember me next spring, let's make a test. If I can ask you a question about something that happened in your life and you can't remember, then you must come with me tomorrow."

"Agreed," said Old Hark. "Ask away."

Death closed the ledger and put his pen away. He smiled again and asked, "On your second birthday, your mother baked up a special treat. What was it?" Then Death turned and walked off toward the forest path. "Good day," he called. "I'll see you tomorrow."

18

It began to snow. Old Hark returned to his cabin, kicked the snow off his boots and went inside. He put on some coffee to perking and sat back in his rocking chair. He sat there for hours, remembering many things, many smells, and tastes, and sounds, and people, but of course he couldn't remember what his mother baked special on his second birthday.

Some birds chirped outside the door. The snow had stopped. Old Hark got a handful of feed, opened the door and chucked it out. The birds made a fuss of noise, but just as Old Hark closed the door, he heard one chirp above and unlike any of the others, a very strange chirp.

It sounded exactly as if one of the birds had said, "Plumcakes."

21

It snowed most of the night. Next morning, Old Hark made his rounds to the bird feeders and scattered plenty of feed. He got his shovel and a ladder out then and climbed up to shove some of the snow off the roof of the cabin.

While he was up there, Death came around with his ledger under his arm. He stood next to the ladder and shouted out a cheery "Good morning!" Old Hark looked down. He put a finger to one of his nostrils, blew his nose in the snow, and then said, "Plumcakes," and turned back to his work.

That was a surprise for Death. He had spent half the night working on the book. He was tired, and now he was angry and was tempted to pull the ladder out from the old man. But he remembered the words in the book, "Quiet, gentle, peaceful," and he got hold of himself.

"Very good," Death said. "I don't think there's one man in a thousand who could have remembered that far back. But of course it might have been luck. Perhaps you just made a guess at it."

"I didn't guess," Old Hark said.

"But you couldn't do it again," Death said.

"I reckon I could."

"Then just to be absolutely positive it wasn't a guess, let's try it one more time."

"One more time," Hark agreed. "Ask away."

"Very well," said Death. "The question is this. On your first birthday, your mother picked some wild flowers and put them in your crib with you. What kind of flowers were they?" And he walked away up the forest path.

After clearing the roof, Old Hark took his shovel to work on some drift that was leaning onto his fence. Now and then he threw some feed out of his pocket to the birds that followed him about. There was singing and chirping around the fence, and as he finished up and headed back to the cabin, Old Hark heard in back of him an unusual chirp, loud and clear.

It sounded exactly as if one of the birds had said, "Buttercups."

29

Next morning when Death came around, Old Hark was under his lean-to splitting wood.

"Good morning," Death said lightly, although actually he was feeling grouchy because he had been up half the night fixing his book to fit the old man into a new place.

Old Hark spit on his hands and took a fresh grip on his splitting maul. "Buttercups," he said, and swung the maul.

Death swallowed hard to keep from crying out. It was impossible. He would have liked to have Old Hark's wedge jump up and crack his skull, but of course that wasn't in the book. Slowly, Death got control of himself.

"Amazing," Death said. "I can scarcely believe it. What a memory. I'm astounded, really I am. You don't *suppose* you could possibly do that again? I hardly *believe* you could."

Old Hark took a breath and leaned on the butt of his splitting maul. "I reckon I just might," he said. "But supposing I do? Then you got to let me be all the way into next spring."

"Agreed," Death said. "Agreed. Then it's a wager. One more question. If you can answer, then I won't come again until next spring. If you can't answer . . . well, then . . ." Death made a check mark in the air.

"Ask away," said Old Hark.

"The question is this," said Death. "On the day you were born, when the midwife held you up in the air, what were the first words your father said?" Death cocked his head, smiled, and walked away.

After splitting the wood, Old Hark filled all the bird feeders and broke up the ice in the cistern. All the while he was paying close attention to the birds which always fluttered nearby, but he heard nothing out of the ordinary in their chirping. Then he went inside. He stoked up the fire, made coffee, took a nap and puttered with some harness. But every now and then he opened the door and threw out some feed, and listened carefully. Just ordinary singing and chirping. He was feeling especially tired and went to bed early with no answer to the question.

Now the reason the birds could tell him nothing was this. Old Hark had been born in that very cabin, and generations of birds had known him and everything about him, and because of their love for the old man they had passed on many memories of him, and so they knew the answers to the other questions.

35

But on the day the old man was born, in the very bed in which he now lay, the window was closed and the curtain was drawn, so the birds knew nothing of what his father's first words were upon seeing his newborn son. They could not help him.

Old Hark woke late, which wasn't like him. His bones hurt, and he felt tired. It took him much longer than usual to get his chores done, and the wind seemed to chill him to the heart. Still, he listened carefully to the birds. They said nothing special. Early in the afternoon, without coffee or even a bite to eat, he undressed and got back into bed. He had never felt quite so tired in his life. Through his half-closed eyes, he watched the birds on his windowsill hopping about, but he was too tired even to crack the window a bit so he could hear them sing. Now and then he fell asleep.

Death knocked on the door in the late afternoon.

"Come in," Old Hark whispered.

"Hello?" Death said, opening the door. Then he saw Old Hark laid out in the bed and understood at once that the old man had no answer to the question.

"Well, well," Death said, taking a chair next to the old man's bed and opening his book on his lap. "Now isn't that more like it, yes indeed. Ha, ha. You old rascal, I've been up half the night again on your account, you know, but it's quite all right now, yes indeed. It's good to see you lying there so quiet and gentle and . . ." Death glanced at the book. ". . . so peaceful."

Old Hark paid him no attention. He was watching the birds playing on the windowsill.

39

"Now," said Death, taking out his pen. "I've managed to fit you in for sunset. Oh, you should appreciate that. It's a choice spot, really. Very appropriate, very . . . *fitting* to the occasion, you know. Daylight ending, the sun going down, darkness coming on. . . . Ah, yes, a choice spot—we usually reserve it for poets." Death ran a finger down the page. "Here we are," he said cheerfully. He took the cap off his pen and moved to make a check mark after Old Hark's name. Then he paused.

"Oh, yes," Death said. "It's a formality, but I must ask you so as to make it all strictly legal. As I recall then, the question was this: On the day you were born, when the midwife held you up in the air, what were the first words your father said?"

But Old Hark had not even been listening. He was looking at the birds, and he said to Death, "Open the window."

Death thrust his head forward and clutched at his pen.

"What did you say?"

"Let the birds sing."

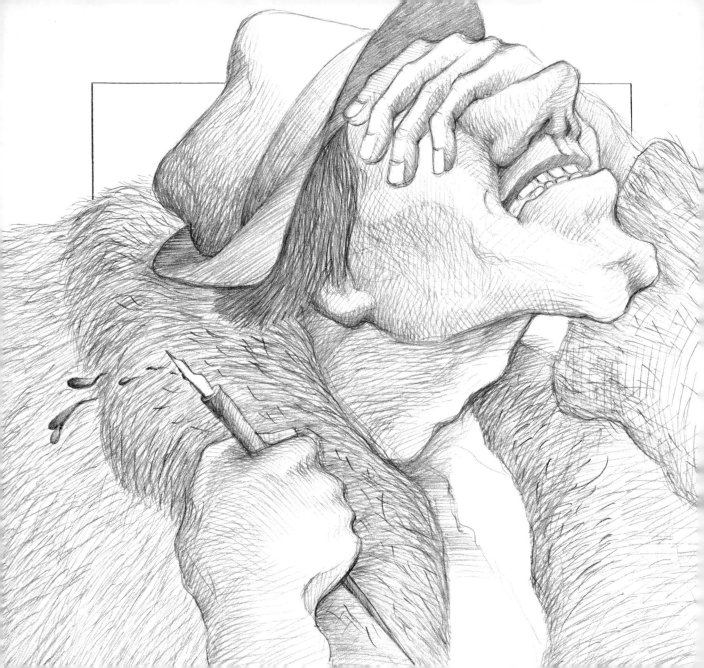

"NOOOOOoooooooo!" Death bellowed. He flung his arms about hysterically, splattering ink, then screamed out again and fell off his chair in a fit. He got up in a rage and pitched his book through the window.

Birds flew in, singing. Death grabbed a handful of his coatfront and threw himself out the window and went stumbling up the forest path.

Old Hark leaped out of bed and watched Death disappear into the forest. He was feeling much better. He put on a wool shirt and got some coffee to perking, then cut himself some cheese and bread. In a short time he figured out what all the commotion had been about.

Of course what it was, is this: Death had lost the wager and must leave Old Hark to live until spring, for his father's first words on seeing his newborn son had been "Open the window! Let the birds sing!"

47